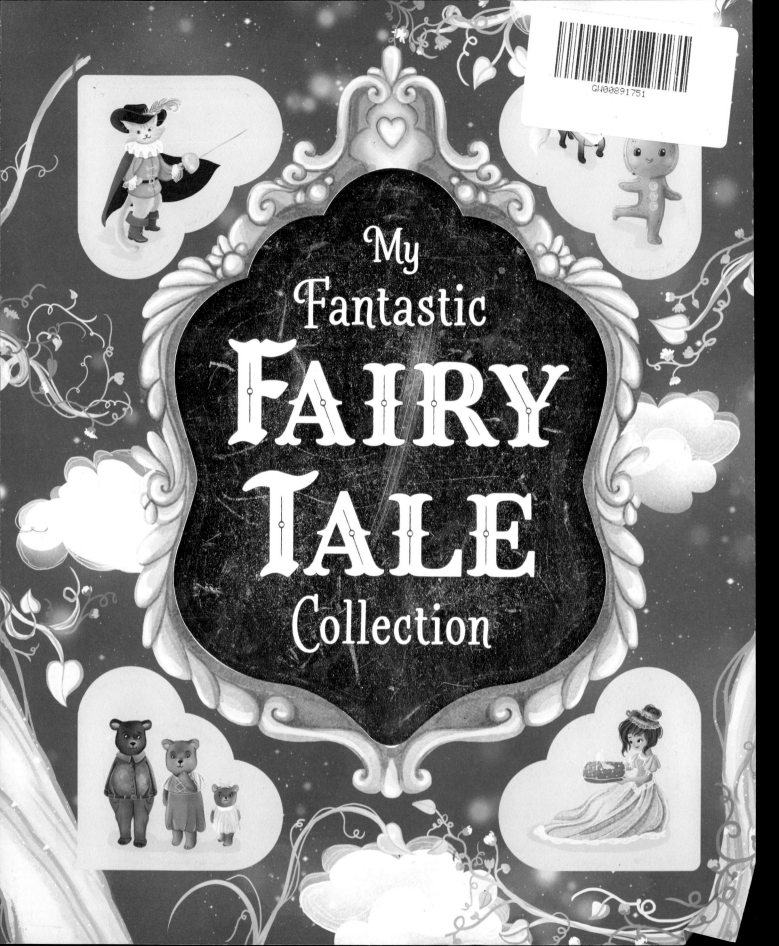

My Fantastic FAIRY TALE Collection

This igloo book belongs to:

....

igloobooks

Published in 2019
by Igloo Books Ltd, Cottage Farm, Sywell, NN6 0BJ
www.igloobooks.com

Copyright © 2019 Igloo Books Ltd
Igloo Books is an imprint of Bonnier Books UK

0919 001.01
2 4 6 8 10 9 7 5 3 1
ISBN 978-1-78905-485-9

Original stories retold by Stephanie Moss
Illustrated by Emanuela Mannello

Cover designed by Hannah George
Interiors designed by Hannah George and Bethany Dowling
Edited by Stephanie Moss

Printed and manufactured in China

Contents

Beauty and the Beast

There once was a poor merchant who had to leave his home to go on a long journey. He asked his youngest daughter, Beauty, if she would like him to bring anything back for her.

"The only gift I desire is a single rose," replied the kind girl.

When the merchant finally travelled home, a terrible storm blew as he made his way back through the deep, dark woods. Rain **poured**, thunder **crashed** and it wasn't long before the merchant was completely lost. As he looked for shelter, he discovered a secret castle at the edge of the forest.

Knock-knock went the weary merchant on the door, and he finally pushed it open. **Creak**! "Hello?" he called, but no one answered. Inside, he noticed a **crackling** fire and a table laid with a splendid feast. Hungry from his travels, the merchant ate as much delicious food as he could.

After warming up by the fire, the merchant was eager to finish his journey home, so he left the castle.

On his way out, he discovered a **beautiful** rose garden. He remembered his promise to his daughter and, as he picked a single, perfect bloom, he heard a **terrifying** roar.

A **hideous** beast appeared before the merchant. The Beast lived in the castle and the beautiful rose garden belonged to him.

"You steal from me after the kindness I have shown you?" growled the Beast. The merchant **begged** for forgiveness, but the Beast was angry.

The Beast locked the merchant in his **cold**, **dark** dungeon and swore he would keep him as his prisoner forever. Far away from the castle, Beauty was very worried that her father had not returned, so she set out to find him. Eventually, she too discovered the Beast's castle.

Beauty was **horrified** when the Beast told her he had
taken her father prisoner for stealing a single rose.
"Take me instead," she demanded, and the Beast agreed.

He treated Beauty with kindness and
they spent many long evenings together.
Soon, the Beast fell in love with Beauty.

Although Beauty became very fond of the Beast, she missed her father terribly.

"You can visit him for one week," said the Beast. With that, he gave Beauty a **magic** mirror that allowed her to see the castle from wherever she was.

Then he put a wishing ring on her finger, and said a **sad** goodbye.

The merchant was overjoyed to see Beauty. Soon, she forgot all about her promise to return to the Beast's castle after one week. Then one night, Beauty looked in the magic mirror and saw the Beast lying motionless. She wished to be with him and, in an **instant**, she was.

Beauty found the Beast **sobbing** and **heartbroken**.
"I love you and I will never leave you again," said Beauty.

Suddenly, the Beast turned
into a **handsome** prince.
Long ago a witch had cast a
spell on him, and Beauty's
love for him had broken it.

Soon after, they were married
at the Beast's castle and they
both lived **happily ever after**.

Puss in Boots

There once was a poor miller's son who owned nothing besides his cat. One day, to the boy's surprise, the cat **spoke** to him!

"Master, if you give me a pair of boots, I promise to turn you into a prince," said the cat. So the boy did as his cat asked.

First, the cat caught some rabbits for the king.
When the king asked who his master was, the cat replied,
"The Marquis of Carabas!" The cat knew his master was really
the miller's son, but he wanted to impress the king.

The clever cat's plan worked straight away, and the
king declared, "Then my daughter shall marry your master!"

Now that the king believed the miller's son was the Marquis of Carabas, he wanted to meet him at once.

Meanwhile, the clever cat ran home. "**Master, you must stand in the river without any clothes on,**" he said. Then, when the royal coach passed by, he called for help.

"The Marquis of Carabas was bathing in the river," he cried, "and someone has stolen his clothes!"

Thinking the unclothed miller's son was indeed the Marquis of Carabas, the king dressed him in fine clothes. Then, he invited the miller's son into the royal coach where the princess was sitting, and they fell in love **instantly**.

Next, the cat ran ahead of the coach to an ogre's castle.
"Can you really transform yourself into different animals?" he asked.

The ogre **magically** turned into a **huge** lion.

"But what about a tiny mouse?" asked the cat.

The ogre did just as he was challenged, but was quickly...

... **gobbled up** by the cat!

When the king arrived, he thought he was at the Marquis of Carabas's castle, so he offered the miller's son his daughter's hand in marriage.

And so the miller's son married a princess and became a prince, just as his puss in boots promised, and they all lived **happily ever after**.

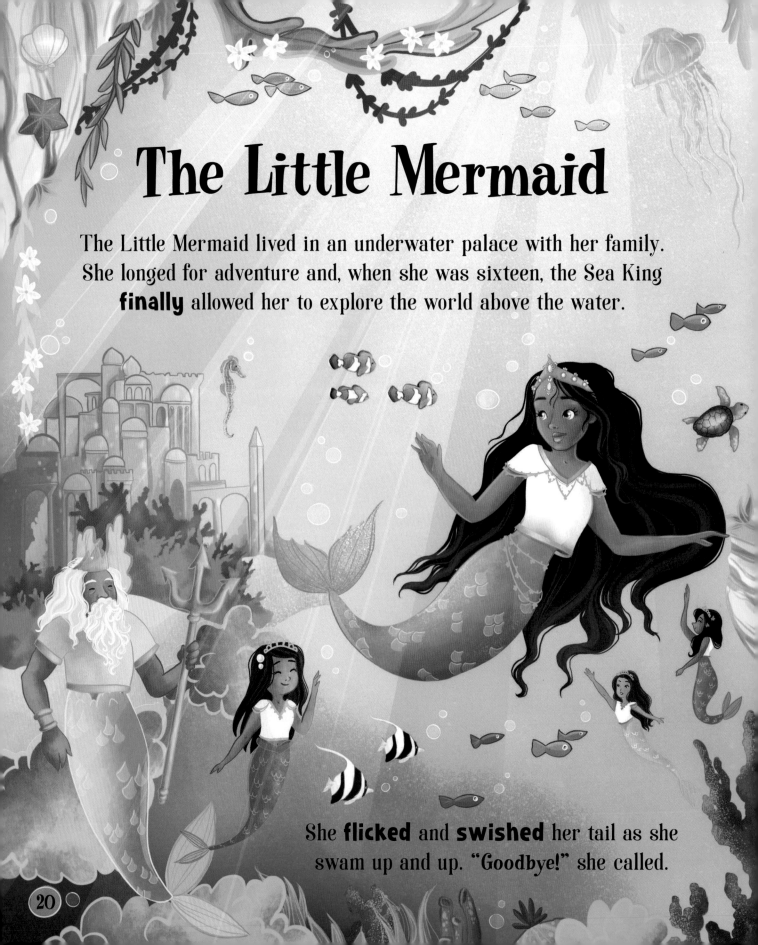

The Little Mermaid

The Little Mermaid lived in an underwater palace with her family. She longed for adventure and, when she was sixteen, the Sea King **finally** allowed her to explore the world above the water.

She **flicked** and **swished** her tail as she swam up and up. "Goodbye!" she called.

Above the waves, the Little Mermaid saw a **beautiful** sunset over a grand ship. As it grew darker, fireworks began to **WHIZZ** and **POP** in the sky.

The people on the ship were having a party for a handsome prince, and the Little Mermaid **instantly** fell in love with him.

Suddenly, thunder **BOOMED** and lightning **FLASHED** as a terrible storm struck. Waves **crashed** over the ship and the prince fell into the deep, dark water. "I must rescue him," said the Little Mermaid. So she dived down into the sea and pulled him safely to shore.

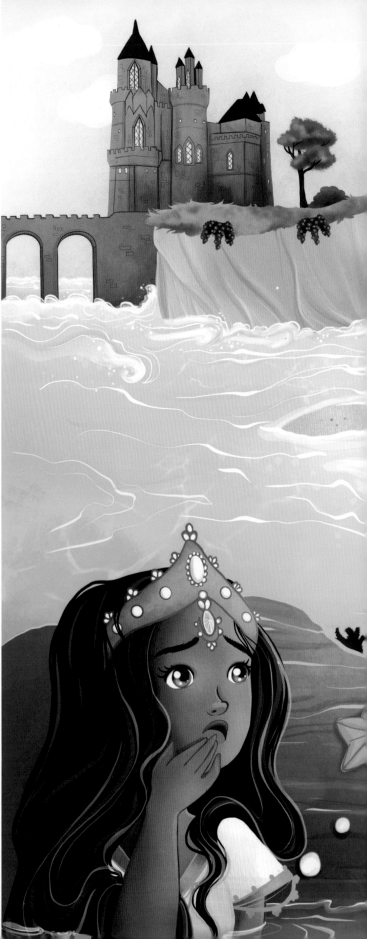

When the storm passed and the prince woke up, the Little Mermaid was waiting nearby, but the prince didn't see her. Instead, a pretty young girl had strolled along the beach, and the prince believed she had saved him.

"No!" gasped the **heartbroken** mermaid, and she returned to the ocean.

23

The Little Mermaid was **desperate** to be with her beloved prince, and she knew only the evil Sea Witch could help. "Drink this potion, and you will become human," she cackled. "But you must give me your voice!" The Little Mermaid finished every drop, and her tail began to change.

By the time she reached the surface, the Little Mermaid had two legs...

... but when she opened her mouth to speak, nothing came out, just as the Sea Witch had promised. Finally, the Little Mermaid found the prince's palace, but she could not tell him who she really was.

Although he didn't know her, the prince was kind to the Little Mermaid. He invited her to stay at the palace and gave her fine clothes to wear.

They often rode through the forest together, as he shared stories with her. **"Maybe he loves me after all,"** the Little Mermaid hoped, silently.

One day, the prince told the Little Mermaid that the king had arranged for him to marry a princess from another land. She was heartbroken all over again, but she could not say a word. So the next day, they sailed together to meet his new bride.

The prince was **overjoyed** when he met the princess, as he recognised her at once. She was the young girl from the beach who he believed had saved him, when in fact it had been the Little Mermaid. **"I was sure I would never see you again!"** he cried, and he declared his love to her.

The Little Mermaid realised she would never be able to tell her prince that she loved him. So she returned to her family, and her tail and voice were restored. "Oh, Father," she sobbed. "You belong here," he said. "One day you will be happy again."

Rapunzel

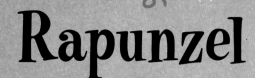

Long ago, there lived a husband and wife who were about
to have a baby. They lived next to a witch who grew
many **delicious** plants in her **magical** garden.

"Please, husband," said the woman, one day,
"will you fetch me some of that tasty rapunzel plant?"

So her kind husband climbed into the witch's garden, but when the witch caught him stealing, she was **furious**.

"You can have the rapunzel," she shrieked, "but in return, you must give me your child when it is born!" Sure enough, the witch took the baby and named her Rapunzel.

Time passed and Rapunzel grew up to be **very** beautiful. She had **golden** hair that was as bright as the sun, and it grew all the way down to the floor. But the witch was **jealous** of her beauty. So she locked Rapunzel in a tall tower in the forest, which had a single window and no doors.

Each time the witch came
to visit, she called,
"Rapunzel, Rapunzel,
let down your hair!"

Rapunzel would let her long,
flowing locks fall out of
the window, all the way to the
ground. Then the witch would
use it like a rope to climb up
the tower. But the rest of the
time, Rapunzel was very lonely.

Rapunzel spent her days singing and her beautiful voice could be heard **echoing** through the forest.

Then one day, a **handsome** prince from another kingdom was riding by and, when he heard Rapunzel singing, he knew he had to meet her. Suddenly, he heard the witch call...

... "Rapunzel, Rapunzel, let down your hair!"

The prince watched the witch climb up Rapunzel's hair and enter the tower through the window at the top.

Then, when he was sure the witch was gone, he did exactly as she had, calling, "Rapunzel, Rapunzel, let down your hair!" Then he climbed up the tower and through the window.

When Rapunzel saw the prince instead of the witch, she couldn't believe her eyes! But the prince was very kind to her and soon, Rapunzel began to fall **deeply** in love with him.

He visited Rapunzel every day in secret, but one day, she mistakenly told the witch everything.

"You are much heavier to pull up the tower than my prince is," said Rapunzel. The witch was so angry that Rapunzel had a secret visitor, she **chopped** off the girl's beautiful hair and banished her into the deep, dark forest.

Then, the prince called, "Rapunzel, Rapunzel, let down your hair!"

The witch threw Rapunzel's chopped-off hair out of the window for the prince to climb up. Then she **cackled** as she let go, and he fell into a tangle of thorns below.

Hurt and bleeding, the prince **stumbled** into the forest. "Where is my Rapunzel?" he cried, but no one answered.

The injured prince wandered from place to place, searching for his true love. At last, he heard **sweet** singing and followed the sound to a pretty glade.

There was Rapunzel and, when she saw her prince, she was **overjoyed**. "I have found you!" cried the prince, and they lived **happily ever after**.

Cinderella

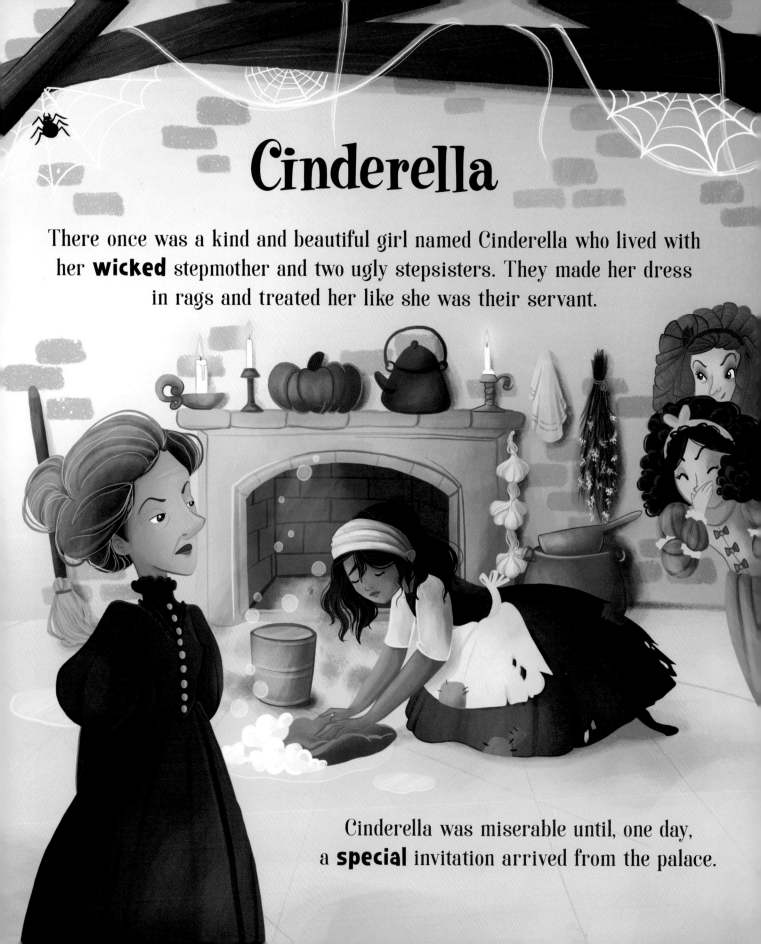

There once was a kind and beautiful girl named Cinderella who lived with her **wicked** stepmother and two ugly stepsisters. They made her dress in rags and treated her like she was their servant.

Cinderella was miserable until, one day, a **special** invitation arrived from the palace.

"There's going to be a royal ball for the whole kingdom!" shrieked the stepsisters. Cinderella couldn't wait to get ready, but her cruel stepmother stopped her.

"Oh, you can't go. You have too many chores to do," she **sneered**. With that, they all left Cinderella **sobbing** by the fireplace.

"I wish I could go to the ball," whispered Cinderella. Suddenly, her fairy godmother appeared outside. "You shall go to the ball!" she said.

With a **swish** of her wand, she turned newts into footmen, mice into horses, and a pumpkin into a **shimmering** carriage. Then, Cinderella's rags became a **glittering** ballgown...

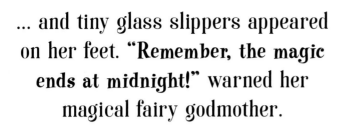

... and tiny glass slippers appeared on her feet. "Remember, the magic ends at midnight!" warned her magical fairy godmother.

When Cinderella finally arrived at the ball, the prince thought she was the most **beautiful** girl he had ever seen.

They danced all evening, but when the clock **struck** twelve, Cinderella fled from the palace, leaving only a glass slipper.

43

The **heartbroken** prince promised he would marry the girl whose foot fit the slipper. He searched the whole kingdom until, finally, he reached Cinderella's house. "It's my slipper!" cried each of her stepsisters, but their big feet wouldn't fit.

"Who else lives here?" asked the prince. "I do!" cried Cinderella, **bursting** in.

The slipper fit **perfectly**, and she and the prince were married at once. Cinderella became a princess and she even forgave her wicked family...

... and they all lived **happily ever after**.

Goldilocks
and the
Three Bears

Once upon a time there was a little girl named Goldilocks.
One day, when she was walking in the forest, she came across
a cottage. Little did Goldilocks know, it belonged to a family
of three bears, and they were out for a morning walk.

Knock-knock went
Goldilocks on the door.

When no one answered, Goldilocks pushed open the door and went inside. She saw three bowls of porridge on the kitchen table and, feeling hungry after her walk, Goldilocks sat down and tried some.

"Ow, this porridge is too hot!" she cried,
when she tasted the porridge from the first bowl.

So Goldilocks tried the porridge in the second bowl, but it was too cold.

Finally, she tried the last bowl of porridge. "Ahh, this one is just right," she said, and she **ate** and **ate** until the bowl was clean.

After eating all that porridge, Goldilocks needed a rest.

In the living room, Goldilocks found three chairs.
First was a **big**, wooden chair that was far too tall.

Next was a **squishy** armchair that was far too lumpy.

But the third and smallest one was **perfect**.

However, just as Goldilocks settled down to rest, it broke, **SNAP**, into little pieces!

By now, Goldilocks felt **very** tired indeed,
so she went upstairs to look for the bedroom.

She found three beds which, just like the porridge and chairs, were
all different from each other. When she pulled back the covers
and lay down in the first one, she said, "**This bed is too hard.**"

Next, Goldilocks tried the second bed. **"This one is too soft!"** she said. Then at last, she lay down in the third and final bed.

"Ahh," said Goldilocks, **"this bed is just right."** She was **SO** comfortable that she closed her eyes and fell **fast** asleep.

Meanwhile, the three bears had returned home to their cottage. When they found their porridge had been eaten, they weren't happy **at all**.

"Someone's been eating my porridge," said Daddy Bear.

"Someone's been eating **MY** porridge," said Mummy Bear.

"Someone's been eating my porridge... and **it's all gone!**"

It wasn't long before they realised someone had been in the living room, too.

"Someone's been sitting in my chair," said Daddy Bear.

"Someone's been sitting in MY chair," said Mummy Bear.

**"Someone's been sitting in my chair...
and they've broken it all to pieces!"** cried Baby Bear.

When the three bears finally reached their bedroom,
Daddy Bear said, "Someone's been sleeping in my bed."
Mummy Bear said, "Someone's been sleeping in **MY** bed."

"Someone's been sleeping in my bed... and she's
still there!" shrieked poor Baby Bear.
Goldilocks woke up and saw the three bears.

She was so afraid that she **ran** down the stairs and **fled** out of the cottage. Goldilocks never returned and the three bears never saw her again.

Jack and the Beanstalk

There once was a boy named Jack who lived with his mother. They were very poor and, one day, there was no food left for them to eat.

"You must go to market and sell our cow," said Jack's mother.
Jack was upset, but he did as his mother asked.

On the way to market, Jack met a mysterious man. "I'll give you these magic beans in exchange for your cow," he said. Jack handed over the cow at once, thinking that magic beans sounded very exciting indeed. But when he showed his mother, she was **furious** with him.

"You sold our cow for a handful of beans!" cried Jack's mother. Then she **threw** the beans out of the window and sent Jack to bed.

When he woke up in the morning, Jack couldn't believe his eyes. A **huge** beanstalk had grown in the garden. The beans were magic after all!

Jack couldn't resist climbing the magic beanstalk. He climbed until he was so high up that he found himself in an **enchanted** kingdom above the clouds.

In front of him was a huge castle, with **glittering** gold doors. Jack had just crept inside when he heard **thumping** footsteps.

Jack hid as he watched an **enormous** giant sit down and start counting golden coins onto the table. Suddenly, the giant sniffed the air and bellowed, **"Fee, fi, fo, fum.** I smell the blood of an Englishman! Be he alive, or be he dead, I'll grind his bones to make my bread!"

The giant searched everywhere for Jack, but eventually, he gave up and fell asleep. Then Jack climbed onto the table, took one of the bags of money and **rushed** back to the beanstalk.

"Where have you been?" cried Jack's mother, when he returned home. So he showed her the coins and she was **overjoyed**.

Soon their riches were gone, so Jack climbed the beanstalk again.
He saw a **beautiful** hen on the giant's table, but he heard the giant's
cry once more. "**Fee, fi, fo, fum.** I smell the blood of an Englishman!
Be he alive, or be he dead, I'll grind his bones to make my bread!"

Jack hid, and he watched as the giant started to play a little golden harp.
Suddenly, the hen laid an egg of pure gold. "Wow," whispered Jack.
He tucked the hen under his arm as soon as the giant was asleep, then
tiptoed out of the castle and back towards the magic beanstalk.

At home, Jack tried to make the hen lay a golden egg, but it just **clucked**, sadly. *"We need the golden harp,"* said Jack.

So he climbed the beanstalk one last time and found the harp in one of the giant's cupboards. Then, Jack heard him **bellowing** once more.

"**Fee, fi, fo, fum.** I smell the blood of an Englishman!
Be he alive, or be he dead, I'll grind his bones to make my bread!"

Before the giant could catch him,
Jack **grabbed** the harp and ran to
the beanstalk. But the magical harp
cried out, "Master, I'm being stolen!"

The giant jumped onto the beanstalk and began climbing down, making it **swish** and **sway**.

When Jack reached the bottom, he fetched an axe. He chopped at the beanstalk until it **toppled** down, bringing the mighty giant **crashing** to the ground once and for all.

At last, Jack played the magic harp to the hen and it laid its golden eggs. Jack and his mother were never poor again and they lived **happily ever after**.

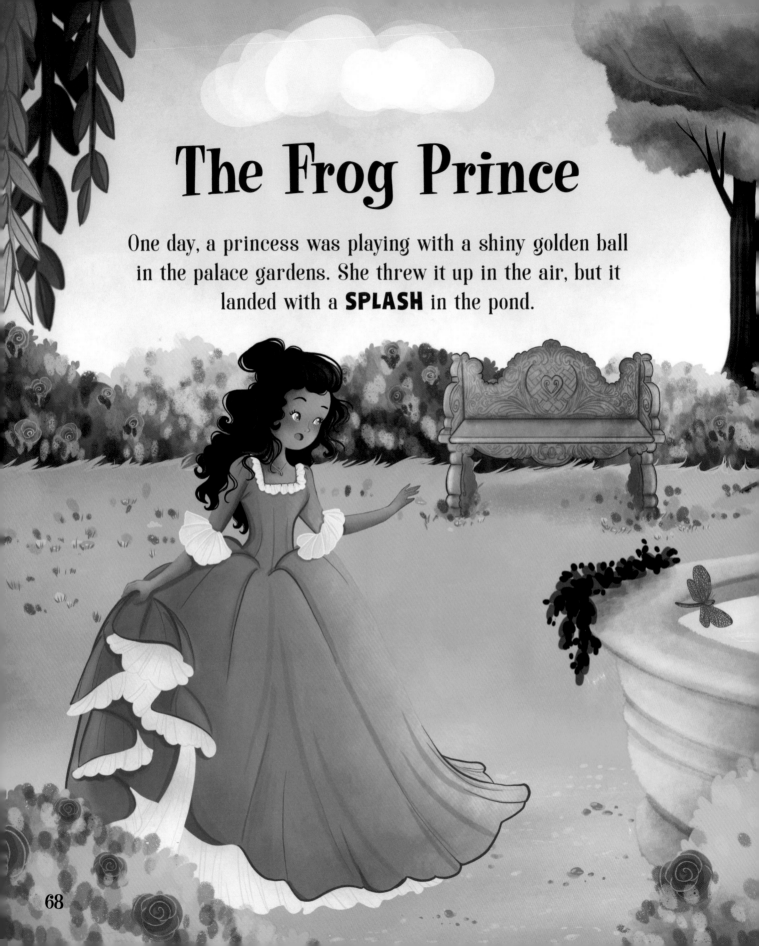

The Frog Prince

One day, a princess was playing with a shiny golden ball in the palace gardens. She threw it up in the air, but it landed with a **SPLASH** in the pond.

68

As she watched the ball sink to the bottom, the princess began to cry. "What's wrong?" asked a voice.

It belonged to a **big**, **ugly** frog, sitting on a lily pad. The princess explained that she had lost her ball.

"I'll get it for you," said the frog, "if you let me sit at your table, eat from your plate, drink from your cup and sleep in your royal bed."

The princess agreed, so the frog dived down to get the ball. But as soon as he had, the naughty princess **grabbed** it from him and ran away! The next day, she had forgotten all about her promise, but the frog had not.

When the frog arrived at the palace for dinner, the princess **shrieked**, but the king said, "**No daughter of mine will break a promise.**" So the unhappy princess let the frog eat from her plate and drink from her cup.

After dinner, the frog yawned and said, "Time for bed!"
The princess **shuddered**, remembering the rest of her promise.

And so the **slimy** frog slept on the soft pillow next to her until the
next morning. "Kiss me goodbye and you will be rid of me forever,"
croaked the frog. So the princess closed her eyes and kissed him.

"Yuck!"

she cried...

... but when she opened her eyes, a **handsome** prince was standing in the frog's place. "A witch cursed me," the prince explained, "and only the kiss of a princess would break her terrible spell."

And of course, they fell in love and lived **happily ever after**.

The Gingerbread Man

One day, a little old woman decided to bake a gingerbread man. She gave him currants for eyes and a little mouth of icing and soon, she was ready to put him in the oven. But much to the woman's surprise, the gingerbread man **jumped** off the baking tray before she could close the door!

He **ran** out of the old woman's house and down the lane, singing...

..."Run, run, as fast as you can.
You can't catch me,
I'm the gingerbread man!"

The old woman started to chase him, and it wasn't long before the gingerbread man reached a field where a cow was **munching** on grass.

"Mmm," said the cow, "you look good to eat." **MOO!**
The cheeky gingerbread man just laughed and kept on running.

He sang,
"Run, run, as fast as you can.
You can't catch me,
I'm the gingerbread man!"

The hungry cow
chased after him, with the
old woman not far behind.

Soon, the gingerbread man reached a farmyard, where a dog was chewing a bone. "Mmm," said the dog, "you look good to eat." **WOOF!**

Still, the gingerbread man kept **laughing** and **singing** as he ran.

"Run, run as fast as you can.
You can't catch me,
I'm the gingerbread man!"

Soon, the dog, the cow and the old woman were all chasing after the gingerbread man. They had nearly caught up, when he reached a river. "Oh, no!" he cried. "How will I **cross the water?**" Then he met a **hungry** fox. "I will **carry you across,**" he said.

So the gingerbread man **jumped** onto his back.
Then the fox said, "**Sit on my head where it is dry.**"
So the gingerbread man did. Then...

... SNAP!

SNAP!

SNAP!

The fox had **tossed** him into the air and swallowed him! And **that** was the end of the gingerbread man.

Hansel and Gretel

Once upon a time, a woodcutter lived with his two children, Hansel and Gretel, and their new stepmother. The family was **so poor** that there was hardly enough food to eat.

"You must take the children into the woods and leave them there," said the children's cruel stepmother one day.

The children overheard their stepmother's plans, and Gretel began to cry, but Hansel had a plan of his own.

When their father led them into the woods the next morning, Hansel **crumbled** up a piece of bread he had put in his pocket. Then he left a trail of breadcrumbs behind him.

When Hansel and Gretel were fast asleep, the woodcutter left them **deep** in the woods and, when they woke up, they were **all alone**.

"Don't worry," said Hansel. "We can follow the trail of breadcrumbs home." But the birds had eaten **every** crumb and the children were soon lost.

Suddenly, a **beautiful** white dove seemed to call to the children. It led them through the woods to an **amazing** gingerbread house! The windows were spun sugar and the roof was dripping with icing.

Hansel and Gretel were **so** hungry, they nibbled at some of the gingerbread walls. "Mmm, **delicious**," said Gretel.

Soon, an old woman appeared. "I have lots more lovely treats inside," she said, with a **twinkle** in her eye.

However, she was really a witch who liked to eat little children and, as soon as they were inside the cottage, she **grabbed** Hansel and **locked** him in a cage.

The witch made Gretel cook for Hansel.

"When you are nice and fat,
I shall cook you for my supper!"
shrieked the witch.

Every day, Hansel held out a chicken
bone through the cage, pretending it was
his finger. The witch, who couldn't see
very well, thought he felt very skinny!

Soon, the witch grew impatient. "I will **cook you anyway, fat or skinny!**" she cried. First, she asked Gretel to climb into the oven to make sure there was room. "**Please, show me how?**" asked clever Gretel.

When the witch peered inside, Gretel **shoved** her in and **slammed** the door shut.

Gretel freed Hansel and they filled their pockets with the witch's secret treasure. "How will we find our way home?" asked Gretel.

Suddenly, the white dove **cooed** softly and the children followed it until they saw their cottage. With their stepmother gone, they forgave their father and were never poor again.

Snow White

There once was a beautiful queen who longed to have a child.
"She will have skin as white as snow and hair as black
as night. I will call her Snow White," she said.

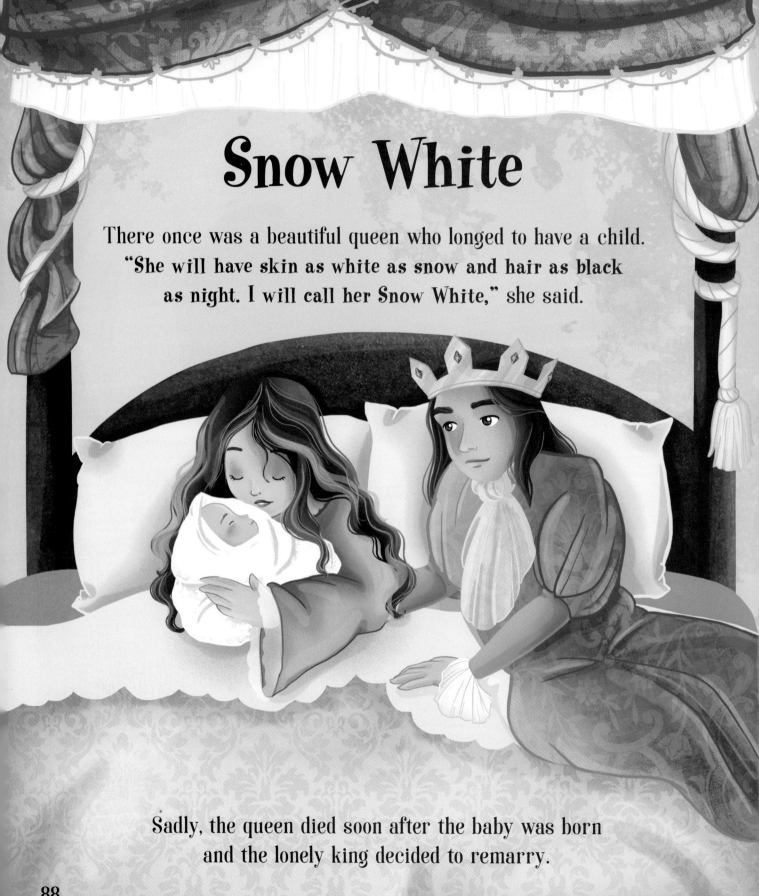

Sadly, the queen died soon after the baby was born
and the lonely king decided to remarry.

The new queen was **cruel** and **jealous**.
She had a magic mirror and every day she asked it,
"Mirror, mirror, on the wall, who **is** the fairest of them all?"
The mirror, which always told the truth, replied
with the same answer each time.

"You are, my queen," it said.

Many years passed and
Snow White grew up to be
a **beautiful** princess.
Her wicked stepmother
became more and more
jealous until, one day,
when she asked the magic
mirror her question, the
reply was different.

"Snow White is the
fairest of them all," it said.

The queen was **furious** and ordered her huntsman to
kill Snow White. But instead, the kind man led the princess
deep into the woods. **"Run away and do not return,"** he said.
Poor Snow White ran through the thorns and brambles
until she saw a pretty little cottage in a clearing.

When Snow White looked inside, she saw seven of everything!

There were seven chairs at the table and seven beds upstairs.

The princess lay down on one of the little beds and fell fast asleep.
When she woke up, there were seven dwarfs staring at her.
"Please let me stay here," she pleaded, and the kind dwarfs agreed.

Snow White was happy with the dwarfs, but her troubles weren't over.
Certain that her beautiful stepdaughter was dead, the queen asked,
"Mirror, mirror, on the wall, who is the fairest of them all?"

"Snow White is the fairest," it replied.
The wicked queen planned her revenge at once.

The queen used her **evil** magic to transform into an old woman.

Then she filled a basket with **poisoned** apples and gave one to Snow White when she was all alone. Not knowing it was her stepmother in disguise, Snow White took a bite and **instantly** fell to the floor in a spell of sleep.

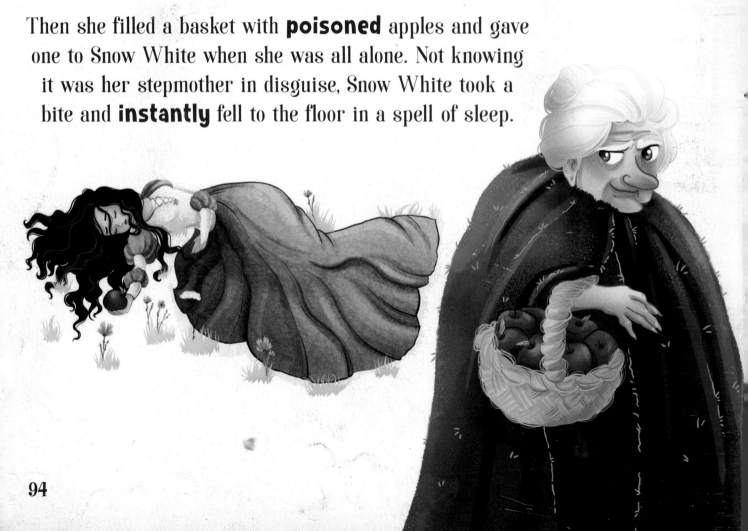

When the dwarfs returned, they found Snow White lying on the ground as if dead. They were very sad and they **wept** for their beautiful princess. They put her to rest in the forest, on a bed covered with glass, so they could watch over her every day. Eventually, a prince rode by.

"What a beautiful maiden," whispered the prince. Thinking Snow White was only sleeping, he bent down to kiss her.

As soon as he did, Snow White woke up and, at the sight of the handsome prince, instantly fell in love with him. The dwarfs were **overjoyed** and everyone lived **happily ever after**.